Art Education

Henry Turner Bailey

Contents

ART EDUCATION

BY

Henry Turner Bailey

EDITOR'S INTRODUCTION

IT is quite unnecessary to argue the worth of art education with those who have experienced beauty fully. To them it is an important value in life, one by which the refinement of human existence is measured. If a large generosity of spirit be coupled with esthetic appreciation, these persons would gladly give every child some training in the creation and appreciation of the quality of beauty. They believe in art training because they would add to the general enrichment of human life.

Unfortunately all are not possessed of an esthetic experience which convinces and a generous spirit which shares. An ignorance which disdains refinement, a poverty which dares not aspire to it, and a selfishness made respectable by aristocratic traditions, — all conspire to sustain the prevalent belief that art is a luxury. Since education is so very common, and art can be made so very cheap, it seems amazing that a people, frankly democratic in aspiration, should have done so little to make the art element common in life. It may be that our particular tradition and history impede us. Doubtless the Puritan tradition in American life has made us partly blind to esthetic values. To some of our people, many forms of art expression are mere frivolities. Play, athletics, dancing, and sociability are often regarded as wasteful and trivial. Again we are not far from our frontier life. America is young. A short while back, we were all pioneers wresting a livelihood from nature under conditions which called for complete attention to economic needs. Now that we are prosperous, that early dominance of economic values still persists to the continued subordination of esthetic considerations. The result is seen in our generally accepted aristocratic conception of art. The rich feel that beauty is a perquisite of prosperity. The poor hardly dare to consider it as their right. The artists themselves, conscious of their best-paying clientage, despite their protestations to the contrary devote a disproportionate amount of their genius and energy to art forms especially adapted to the uses of the prosperous leisure class. Their interest in design applies itself to the composition of portraits far more than to the structure of cups and saucers. They have the defense that creative power must supply the demand of the appreciative. If such be the case, we must develop a democratic art through the bestowal of taste on the multitude. This is the task of art education in the schools.

In a restricted way we have been engaged in art education through the schools for some time. But the results have not been satisfactory. The whole program needs careful criticism and thorough reconstruction.

To begin with, the program for art education in the schools has been narrow and fragmentary, — a small amount of drawing and color work, a little singing, and some literature. And most of the things sung, read, and drawn have been unrelated to the common life. We did not make substantial progress in moral teaching as long as we were content to confine it to the Sunday School or other classroom period. Progress came when morality was treated as an aspect of the child's whole life. Art teaching must undergo a similar evolution. It is well enough to teach art in special class periods in connection with special subjects. It is better to care for art everywhere in school life. Life at school is full of unused opportuni-ties for art teaching. One has only to look at the school premises to appreciate this fact. But it is probable that the program must create opportunities not now existent in school life. Festivals, dramatizations, dancing, and other esthetic expressions of sociable life require fuller opportunity than the school provides.

Then the school's whole theory of transmitting art from classroom to adult life will need to be changed. The present belief is that the child can be put through adult ways of doing things and, finally, when he has become a full-fledged member of society, be counted an art devotee. The futility of such dogma has already been made apparent in intellectual teaching. Its futility is even more obvious when applied to the training of the sensibilities. The only way to become thoroughly intellectual or esthetic is to observe rational or artistic standards in one's own absorbing affairs. Then as affairs enlarge from the narrow boundaries of childhood into the wide world itself, the methods of a logical or esthetic life are extended. Beauty, like morals and rationality, must be made the daily and ubiquitous habit of school life. School life, properly conducted, is the child's own life. As adults will be expected to keep beautiful their temples of government, their habitations, their parks and streets, the children must from the start be held responsible for art in their own institutions. The grounds, the gardens, the schoolroom, the conduct of sociability, —are all their own. As men often gather in a formal way to discuss the beautifying of their city, the children will come together in the art period to learn the manner of making their own domain more attractive. The formal study of art so many periods a week is important, but it is fruitless without the thought of realizing beauty in the child's immediate life.

Finally, the aim of art education needs modification. The first teachers of drawing and music were largely professional artists. They trained future mechanics, farmers, and merchants as though they were all destined to belong to an artistic profession. The interest of students was killed with prolonged practice in a technique that they did not require in the constructions and expressions of their own lives. Meanwhile the opportunity to develop appreciation had passed. By way of extreme reaction against this point of view, many now urge that art education should aim exclusively at art appreciation, artistic power being completely subordinated as a purpose. There is probably much sanity in this extreme reform. To be sure, most people will control the esthetic quality of their lives through the exercise of choice among other men's creations; but there is always need and opportunity for artistic construction in every man's life. Hence it should not be completely omitted. Again, it must be remembered that little children learn best through active experiences, and artistic expression with them may thus be a pedagogical means rather than an end. As they grow older they will gain a further development of appreciative taste, through personal choice operating among varied opportunities.

It was with such convictions as the above in mind that a monograph on art education has long been sought for this series. It is with a sure appreciation that the treatment needed is here provided that the following is offered. If only it can be got into the minds, as well as the hands, of teachers, it will aid greatly in the widespread reform of our art teaching.

FOREWORD

CAN rules or tutors educate The semigod whom we await? He must be musical, Tremulous, impressional, Alive to gentle influence Of landscape and of sky And tender to the spirit-touch Of man's or maiden's eye: But, to his native centre fast, Shall into Future fuse the Past, And the world's flowing fates in his own mould recast.

EMERSON.

ART EDUCATION I ITS AIM AND METHOD THE purpose of art education is the development of appreciation for the beautiful and of power to produce beautiful things. Such taste and skill will not appear when the teacher stamps his foot. They are fruits. They must be grown. The seeds that will produce them are in the heart of every normal child. Sometimes these seeds are of such potency that they will sprout and bring forth fruit under what seem to be the most adverse conditions; but our whole theory of education rests on the conviction that conditions can and should be controlled and utilized. We believe that if the rocks be removed, the thorn-bushes burned, and the hard-trodden soil broken up, the seeds will be more likely to produce the hundredfold. Taste develops gradually through the making of choices with reference to some ideal. Skill

ART EDUCATION

develops slowly through doing things with reference to some standard of excellence. In art education, therefore, every possible opportunity should be given for those conditions and activities through which taste and skill may mature.

This means, first, beautiful school buildings and grounds.

II
THE SCHOOL ESTATE A FACTOR

A BEAUTIFUL school estate, large or small, in city or in country, means an estate that appears adequate and consistent. The building should be one of the best in town — better than the average home of that town — and well placed in an ample lot. The lot should be large enough to admit of a spacious playground and a lawn with shrubs and flowers. If both the playground and lawn are impossible, the playground is preferable. The beauty that appears in the faces of healthy, happy children at play is finer and more desirable than that guarded by " Keep-off-the-grass" signs.

But both are never quite impossible. Even in cities with paved courts, ivy may grow upon brick walls, veiling them with life, a life that weaves a fresh pattern every spring and a more richly colored one every fall. And in the smallest yard there is room for one tree at least, one colony of active tenants working wonders in handicraft — buds, leaves, blossoms, fruit, for the delight of seeing eyes. Perhaps room cannot be found upon the ground for even one flower garden; but room can always be found in the windows. If the janitor is such an ogre that window gardens cannot thrive inside the schoolroom, for six months at least they can thrive outside the window. Nature will be gracious to them. One of the delights in German cities is the loveliness of the window-gardens. The best of these are often in the civic buildings, the city hall, the court-house, the police station, the public school.

Boxes of wood made to fit the window-ledge, and lined with zinc, or better, with copper, to retain moisture, and painted to harmonize with the colors of the building, may become a source of delight to the children and to the public. Planning the boxes, measuring, estimating, making the wooden part, ordering the lining (if it cannot be produced at school), painting the boxes, learning how to fill them, plant them, care for them, and how to get the greatest amount of enjoyment out of what they produce, — these activities constitute a series of first-class exercises having art-educational value.

If the school lot is extensive, and lawns and gardens are possible, they should be cared for by the children, under supervision.

We forget that in forty years the children now in school will be the owners of the town. Ought the town of that day to be a place of parks and boulevards, of handsome civic buildings, attractive places of business, and delightful homes? Then the children in the schools now must be led to feel that they are already citizens of the town beautiful, cooperating factors in producing ideal conditions everywhere, beginning in the yard of their own school. The making of a plan of the grounds to scale, the location of the grass-plots, walks, and gardens, the preparation of the soil, the ordering of the shrubs and seeds, the planting of these, the care of the growing things, are all art-educational projects. Moreover the offering of a half-hour outdoors for mowing the lawn or weeding the garden would do more to stimulate the mental activities of certain pupils indoors than would a bunch of birch twigs brought into the schoolroom.

The point is that a good school building, happily at home in its well-cared-for lot, gives the children an ideal with which to compare their own homes and begins to develop taste; and that participation in the production and conduct of such a thing means the doing of something worth while with reference to a standard of excellence, and makes for skill.

III
THE SCHOOLROOM A FACTOR

THE ideal schoolroom for a kindergarten or first primary grade is large, well lighted, with an agreeable soft color upon the walls. It is properly heated and ventilated, and has in addition a place for an open fire, an aquarium, a canary bird, a window garden, and a piano. A few well-chosen casts and pictures adorn the walls. A case of accessible books, a cabinet of illustrative material, and a supply-closet are also essential. The furniture includes a sand-table and a work bench. In the upper grades some of these things can be dispensed with, and other things must be added. In every grade the ideal is a handsome, convenient workroom, so well designed, so perfectly cared-for, that its every element is delightful and educational to the children of that grade.

Little children ought to feel all that an open fire can give on a dull, chill day when rain is falling or snow is driving. Whittier's "Snow- Bound," and many another choice bit of literature will then mean more to them. They ought to hear the sweet, joyful gush of melody from a canary's throat, and see the bird produce it. Birds and bird songs and good music of every kind will seem dearer to them after such an experience in early childhood. An intimate acquaintance with the life history of a few flowers, the handling of a few choice books, familiarity with a few of the best works of fine art, each year in school, are all illuminating and potent experiences which every child should have. The opportunity in every grade for children to express themselves not only vocally, but manually, is an inalienable right that must not be denied. In other words, the schoolroom should furnish ideals and standards of excellence in everything it involves.

The teacher is fortunate who has an ideal schoolroom; but perhaps the teacher is more fortunate who has not, for the opportunity to produce one with the cooperation of the children is not to be despised.

THE SCHOOLROOM A FACTOR

A favorable school equipment

A schoolroom decorated and furnished in such a way that its equipment and appearance are calculated to promote the growth of skill and taste can be achieved in any community by any intelligent and persistent teacher who has won the love of her pupils. To such a teacher all things are possible.

The elements that combine to produce an interior of this kind are the colors of walls, ceiling, and woodwork, the wall and window decorations, and temporary exhibits of various kinds. These may well be considered in order. (I) *The color scheme* . The color scheme of a schoolroom should make the room appear at once cheerful and restful. This effect cannot be secured by the use of brilliant hues or violent contrasts of color.

The colors selected should help to adjust the light which enters the room to the requirements of the eye. If the room is flooded with direct sunlight during school hours, the resulting brilliancy should be somewhat reduced by the use of tones of dull green or cool grays in wall and ceiling. If on the contrary the room receives no sunshine while in use, tints of yellow and orange, very light warm grays, should be used to give a sunny quality to the interior. In such a room the ceiling should be an ivory or cream white to reflect as much warm light as possible. A safe general rule is: Always make ceilings much lighter than walls, but of a hue in harmony with them; paint the woodwork a color similar to that of the walls but slightly darker. If the finish of the room be "natural wood," the colors of the walls must be modified somewhat to bring them into harmony with the finish; or the finish may be modified in color by means of stains, to fit into any desired color scheme.

The one thing to remember is that a fine interior always has a definite tone of its own. It impresses the eye as being an orange, a yellow, a green-yellow, a green, or a blue-green room[1].

If the room receives a large amount of light, the whole scheme of color may be darker than in a moderately lighted room. On the other hand, if the room is not well lighted, the color scheme must be very light in tone.

The best medium for schoolrooms is oil color, fiat finished; that is, treated in such a way that when dry the paint does not have a glassy surface. Surfaces thus colored may be washed whenever necessary

For the windows an easily adjustable, sanitary, and durable shade is the best. If "Venetian blinds" are used, one side may be painted a color to harmonize with the building as seen from the outside, and the other a color to harmonize with the walls of the room as seen from within. If "roller shades" have to be used, they should be selected by experiment with great care. A shade of the wrong color, when the sunlight strikes it, may neutralize or overpower the whole color scheme of the room.

The furniture for a new building can be had in any desired color, and should be ordered toned according to architects' specifications. In an old building the color of the furniture may have to be ignored, unless it is too bad. Then it can be scraped off, and the wood stained and repolished. In color the furniture should be related to the walls by similarity or contrast, but as dark as the finish of the room or even darker in tone.

If a schoolroom is ugly and gloomy in effect, and the school authorities are apathetic or poverty-stricken, a determined teacher may repeat history by appealing directly to the fathers and mothers of the school children. A perfectly definite plan of what is required, tactful requests to some for "moral support," to others for money to purchase materials, and to still others for work, will be sure to be successful. A popular teacher has seldom if ever failed to secure from his district anything

---

1   These terms suggest more intense colors than any school-room should present. They are the names of the key colors, the colors that when mixed with white and other pigments produce soft grays of different hues. These hues may be distinguished from one another in common speech by such terms as yellow-gray, green-gray, etc. In more technical language the colors may be described as hues of one quarter intensity or less.

he has desired for his schoolroom when he has asked in the name of the children.

(2) *Wall decorations* . The walls of the schoolroom should be enriched with works of fine art. These should be chosen with reference to the grade of the children who are to occupy the room, and with reference to the wall spaces and the amount and direction of the light they receive. These decorations are usually pictures or casts, or both.

The first step is to decide what decoration the room requires. Whatever is added should enhance the beauty of the room. This means that everything must appear to be "made for the place," — not too large, not too small, properly lighted, and effective as seen from the seats.

The most important place in the room is of course the wall directly in front of the seated children. This wall is usually without windows and well lighted from the side. Here the chief decoration should be located. One large beautiful picture or cast in a given area is better, as a rule, than many small ones. If more than one seems desirable, all the elements upon the wall should form a pleasing group, with the central element dominant.

A receipt for decorating schoolrooms cannot be given. Each room presents a unique problem, to be successfully solved only by a person of taste; but certain general statements may be made which in every case will be worth considering. (I) Narrow spaces between windows are not good places for pictures, or casts in low relief. (2) Casts in relief demand a strong side light. The lower the relief the more oblique the light should be. (3) A picture presenting but slight contrasts of light and dark demands more light than a picture presenting strong contrasts. The most brilliant picture may therefore be hung on the darkest wall. (4) The mat or frame of a picture should be in harmony with the picture, and of a value darker than the strongest lights of the picture and lighter than its strongest darks. If both mat and frame are desirable, the frame should be darker than the mat. (5) Casts should be framed into the wall or so installed that they appear vitally related in some way to the wall itself. (6) Pictures should be as closely related to the wall as possible. They should not rest upon the top rail of the blackboard and tilt forward into the room. If hung by vertical wires attached near the upper corners of the frame, the picture will hang nearly flat against the wall. Perhaps the best way is to fasten the picture flat against the wall by invisible hangers.

Having determined the number, the size, and the kind of decorations the room requires, the next step is to select the subjects. Here again no receipt can be given. One rule only admits of no exception: Whatever the subject it should be a work of fine art. From among the many pictures and casts of recognized merit, selections should be made appropriate to the grade or purpose of the room. Broadly speaking, little children delight in pictures of animals, of children, and of home life. Older children like pictures which show people at work, pictures full of action, pictures which tell stories easily read. Later, historical pictures, and pictures which express a sentiment, a mood, an aspiration, are more likely to be appreciated. Antique fragments, photographs of ruined temples, famous views of historic sites, do not appeal to children, and should not be forced upon them. In high schools, possibly in upper-grade grammar schools, children should have the opportunity of seeing pictures which deal with the deepest, most significant experiences of life, — pictures like "The Soul Between Doubt and Faith," by Vedder; "The Temptation," by Cornicelius; "He Had Great Possessions," by Watts; "The Golden Stairs," by Burne-Jones; "The Great Good Book," by Miss McChesney. From about the fourteenth to the eighteenth year occurs one of the most critical periods in the development of character. It is the period of transition from the childish to the adult point of view. Experiences begin to take on deeper meaning, ideals begin to emerge, decisions begin to assume greater importance; frequently the spirit gets oriented for life during this period. Pictures of the right sort have been known to be of real value in influencing decisions during these critical years. Their effect in some cases is not immediate; but they are remembered and treasured and have their fruitage in after years. As Emerson says in his "Ode to Beauty" —

"All that's good and great, with thee Works in close conspiracy."

If faithful colored reproductions of masterpieces are to be had, they are more delightful to the younger children than pictures in black and white. Many of the modern large-sized color prints made especially for decorative purposes are excellent. A good carbon photograph, or other facsimile reproduction in black and white, is preferable to a false color print, and for some subjects is ideal. As a rule etchings and fine engravings are out of place on the wall. They do not " carry" well enough to be effective from a distance. They belong in the reference cabinet.

If casts in the round are used they should be located with reference to favorable lighting, the background against which they appear, and convenience in using the room. They should not be in the way, nor in positions which seem precarious. Usually they demand a well-designed pedestal or wall-shelf. A wall-shelf supporting a cast should appear adequate. The solid mass of a cast does not look well supported upon a thin-edged shelf with cast-iron brackets beneath it The effect of the whole should be consistently solid throughout.

Narrow spaces between windows may sometimes be made attractive by means of hanging pots of plants, or (if the room is to be used at night) by small, well-designed fixtures for lights. The danger is always in the direction of over-decoration; and such spaces are usually better left blank.

In a favorable schoolroom the attention of the children should be directed to the color scheme and the decorations, as occasion serves, and reasons should be educed for the presence of the various elements and their interrelations. The room will then become an intelligible object lesson, a recognized standard of excellence, in the light of which other interiors will appear as better or worse. During the last twenty-five years more than a million dollars has been expended in the United States for pictures and casts for schoolroom decoration. Of this amount probably less than five per cent has come from the public funds. The money has been secured from local private purses largely through the efforts of enlightened teachers.

(3) *Temporary exhibits* . The development of taste and skill may be further stimulated by means of beautiful things placed temporarily on exhibition in the schoolroom. Among these are flowers and other plant forms; vases and other examples of fine craftsmanship.

(4) *Flower arrangements* . Children love flowers, and in the country especially often bring them to the schoolroom. Through the cooperation of the teacher this instinctive activity may become the source of perennial delight and of growth in power to produce beauty. A place should be reserved — upon the teacher's desk, or on a stand, or shelf, where the light falls at a favorable angle — for the display of good flower arrangements throughout the school year. Such arrangements will include not only "flowers" in the ordinary sense, but all the beautiful decorative material the plant world affords. When school opens in September, the goldenrod should be supplemented with the ripened grasses and sedges, and sprays of berries. In October the asters and the ripened leaves of rich color should appear in the

schoolroom. In November, sprays of seed-pods and of the late-fruiting shrubs; in December, sprays of the evergreens. During the other winter months, sprays from bushes and trees which retain seed-packs and dried leaves will furnish bouquets of rare beauty. All these should be selected and arranged with the utmost care, in appropriate receptacles, that their beauties may be seen to the best advantage. The children should cooperate in this to the fullest possible extent. Some teach-ers ap-point committees, of two pupils each, to secure and arrange bouquets at certain times. Each committee must be able to give good reasons for the selection of the vase and for the way the sprays are adjusted to it, both as to form and color. In the early spring pots of crocuses, hyacinths, and tulips nurtured by the children indoors will precede the bouquets of wild flowers. Lastly, in April, May, and June will ap-pear sprays of the blossoming trees.

The children should be led to see the wisdom of certain generalizations con-cerning flower arrangement: (I) A group should be limited to one kind of flower and its foliage[2]

(2) Sprays

(3) Sprays whose chief beauty is the beauty of color may be massed; sprays whose chief beauty is a beauty of form should not be arranged in such a way that that beauty is obscured[3].

(4) The receptacle should not vie with that which it holds; it must appear of secondary importance. (5) The arrangement should present a chief center of inter-est with one or more subordinate centers. (6) The arrangement should appear to be balanced rather than bisymmetrical. (7) A single growingplant, brought to perfec-

---

2   This is a rule for beginners. If two kinds are used the rule is, "Each the other adorning." The group should present elements which contrast with one another and yet have something in common. For example, large sprays of wild roses with meadow rue. The "flowers" of the rue are almost like the stamens of the roses in both form and color, and therefore in harmony with them. Properly grouped with the roses, they suggest a filmy cloud about them, like a bridal veil
look best when arranged in positions which suggest their natural growth.
3   Pansies and peonies, for example, are color plants. Masses of them are rich and splendid. Easter lilies are form plants. A single vigorous flowering stalk, with its exquisitely graceful leaves and flow-ers, is bouquet enough. The finest beauties of lilies are lost in a crowd.

tion of form by human skill and taste is the ideal floral decoration[4]

Exercises in floral arrangement are capable of yielding more profitable returns with a majority of pupils than exercises in original design with conventionalized plant forms.

(5) *Mounted pictures* . For convenience pictorial art may be subdivided as "Illustrative Art" and "Fine Art." Illustrative art has as its aim the making of something clearer, more vivid, more attractive than it would otherwise be. It exists for the sake of that something. Fine art has as its aim beauty — "Its own excuse for being." This classification is broad, and hardly scientific; for an illustration may be beautiful, a veritable work of fine art, like Rubens's "Descent from the Cross," in Antwerp Cathedral. On the other hand, some works of fine art — Rodin's "John Baptist," for example — are not beautiful in the ordinary sense. In a general way, however, in illustration the story is of first importance; in fine art, *the way of telling* the story. Illustration corre-

sponds roughly with prose; fine art with poetry. Illustrations are to be consulted; works of fine art are to be contemplated.

Such pictures as a view in a London street or in a harvest-field in Dakota; a portrait of the German Emperor or of Holmes; a photograph of a group of palm trees or of a bouquet of prize roses, come under the head of "Illustrative Art," and should be kept in the closet for occasional use. Such pictures as Corot's "Spring," Alexander's "Walt Whitman," a garden by Maxfield Parrish, or a fish by Jakuchiu, are works of fine art, worthy of daily companionship. Such pictures cannot all be hung permanently upon the walls of the schoolroom. They may be included, however, in the school's collection of masterpieces. Such a collection every school should acquire.

The making of a school picture gallery is one of the most delightful art-educational activities yet discovered. The method of procedure is as follows: —

(a) With the assistance of the children the teacher begins to gather sheets of

---

4 Left to itself outdoors, the plant's aim is not primarily beauty, but self-preservation and perpetuation of species. To be a *decorative* success, usually it must be relieved of its other responsibilities and instructed by man, so to speak, before it can realize his ideal of beauty for beauty's own sake. But fre quently a plant that has had its own way outdoors, a violet growing in an open pasture, a dandelion amid short grass, an isolated dump of sedge, when transplanted entire into a proper receptacle, will present an arrangement of extraordinary beauty.

cardboard, any size and any color — white, black, brown, gray, etc. — suitable for mounting pictures.

(b)   With the assistance of the children, the teacher begins to gather pictures of all kinds. The best are likely to come from the current magazines, from the advertising literature of book publishers and picture dealers, and from "art publications.[5]"

(c)From these pictures the best, the most beautiful in composition and in color, are selected, by vote of the children (under the wise guidance of the teacher), for the school gallery.

(d)   The selected picture is carefully trimmed to its edge, or to within a sixteenth inch of its edge, and tried upon various sheets of cardboard until the one is discovered upon which the picture ap-pears to best advantage. One picture may require a light mount, another a dark one; one may look best on a warm gray, another on a cool gray, or a green gray. As a general rule the mount should repeat softly, echo, the dominant hue of the picture as a whole or of some important color in it But sometimes the mount should contrast with the picture. The right color can always be determined by experiment. The picture is the song, the mount its accompaniment. The two should go together perfectly.

(e) Having determined the color, the size of the mount is the next consideration. Some pictures demand a wide mount, some a narrow one. This, too, can be determined by experiment. The simplest implements are: two L's of gray cardboard about 12 by 15 inches in size. With one of these in the normal position (L) and the other reversed (Γ) rectangles of any shape and size (up to 12 by 15 inches) may be produced at will by slipping one over the other. The picture to be mounted should be laid on the selected cardboard, the L's placed about it, and moved until the most flattering size and shape of mount is discovered. A vertical picture, a picture in which the height exceeds the width, demands a vertical mount: a horizontal picture, one in which the width exceeds the height, demands a horizontal mount; a square or a circular picture demands a mount nearly square. Owing to a habit of the eye which demands satisfaction, the width of the mount at the top of the picture should always be less than the width of the mount at the bottom of the picture.

5   Good reproductions especially prepared for schools may be purchased, of course. In any case the children should have some part in securing them.

(f) The mount should now be cut to the proper size, and the picture fastened to it, in the predetermined position, by means of good paste of some sort. The paste should be applied along the top edge or upper corners only, or at the four corners, or all over the back of the print, as the print seems to require. The less paste the better, so long as the picture lies flat and is securely fastened.

(g) The name of the picture, the name of the artist, the source of that particular print, and such other information as may seem desirable, including the date, should be written plainly upon the back of the mount.

The growth of such a collection will be gradual, but the pupils' joy therein will be perennial.

Upon a simple easel of wood, so designed that when in use it is practically invisible (as it stands upon the teacher's desk or the exhibition shelf), one picture from the school gallery should be on exhibition every day. The picture for the day should be selected for some good reason. It may be associated with the season, with some school topic, with some local event; or it may be the one best loved by the children at that particular time (their tastes often change rapidly), or one that they do not quite understand as yet. In any case it should be the subject of "warm personal regard" when displayed; otherwise its cultural value is likely to be below par.

(6) *Exhibitions of handicraft* . In every community are people of taste in whose homes are small objects of rare beauty — a box in cloisonne from Japan, a vase of bronze from China, a fan of carved wood from India, a Tanagra statuette from Greece, a bit of mosaic from Italy, a porcelain figurine from Germany, a hand-wrought jewel from France, a piece of lace from Belgium. A teacher of established reputation can always secure such objects for the children to see. The kind of people who care for such things are the kind of people who are always glad for an opportunity to give others, especially the children, the pleasure of seeing them. They will lend one object at a time, for a single day, if the teacher will call for it and return it safely. More fruitful subjects for genuine art education it would be difficult to find. The research work in geography and history, the study of materials, and processes, preliminary to an intelligent look at such a thing as a statuette from Herculaneum, would fill many an hour with vital enthusiastic educative activity.

Here again the wise teacher will not forget that

"Heaven is not reached by a single bound, But we build the ladder by which we rise From the lowly earth to the vaulted skies, And climb to its summit round on round."

For the younger children a quaint toy from Holland is better than a Greek vase; and a grotesque idol from Peru, a far more profitable object of study than an exquisite ivory from Japan.

By means of such temporary exhibits of flowers, pictures, and examples of fine handicraft, daily opportunities may be presented for forming intelligent judgments concerning objects of beauty. Under such conditions taste will often develop with surprising rapidity, and aesthetic enjoyment increase like the light of a new day.

IV
SCHOOL HOUSEKEEPING A FACTOR

THE very heart of beauty is order. Order is purposeful arrangement. The school grounds, the schoolroom and its furnishings have been considered as exemplifying a purposeful arrangement of elements with reference to beauty. Once established, such an order should be maintained by the coöperation of all who participate in the school life. Scratched desks, cut woodwork, littered floors and lawns are incompatible with beauty. So also are disorderly desks and tables; drawers and cupboards. The teacher's desk should present an ideal of orderly arrangement, such as may be reflected in the desk of every pupil. The interior of a drawer or cabinet should present as fine an object lesson. In the school building, at least, there need not be a skeleton in every closet! The secret of satisfactory order lies in the word "purposeful." The order should not be artificial and arbitrary, an order incompatible with daily use, — like the arrangement of books in piles across the four corners of a table. It should be an evidently reasonable order, an order which facilitates use and at the same time satisfies a refined taste. If reference books for the children are kept upon the teacher's desk, for example, they should be placed along the most easily accessible side, in a row, back uppermost, and held by the rack in such a position that the titles may be easily read by the children. The book-rack should be of such a character that it not only holds the books properly but harmonizes with the desk. A cast upon a pedestal is not orderly in relation to the rest of the room if it is in the way. The paths across the school grounds are not in orderly relation unless they are where the children need them. An order determined by convenience and taste is the only aesthetic order. The thought of such an order should be-come habitual in the mind of every pupil.

V
SCHOOL COSTUME A FACTOR

IN every schoolroom the teacher is the supreme center of interest. Not a peculiarity of manner, trick of speech, or habit of thought escapes the keen compound eye of the school. Hence her standard of taste is sure to be discovered and to become a potent influence. In the matter of personal appearance the teacher should be impeccable. Cleanliness, neatness, a becoming coiffure, a simple costume appropriate to her profession and in right relation to her figure and complexion, are absolutely essential. No principle of composition of line, no theory of harmonious coloring should be violated in herself. To live one's aesthetic religion is a duty no less binding than the duty to live one's ethical religion. And the fulfillment of this duty is much easier! It requires a clear perception of one's own excellencies or defects of figure, and of one's natural scheme of color; a conviction that for the sake of the neighbors one should look as well as possible; and a determination to learn what is personally becoming in cut and color, and to adhere to that always.

The teacher who does not possess a knowledge of what is personally becoming could hardly hope to find it in this monograph. The knowledge should be acquired, however, and applied, not only to her own costume but indirectly to that of her pupils. Schools have existed, and will be common one of these days, without the presence of a single inharmoniously dressed pupil. Any teacher of taste and tact can compass such a result by leading her pupils to apply to themselves, from first year to last, their increasing knowledge of color harmony. A hair-ribbon or a necktie, a frock or a coat can be right in color, regardless of cost. To secure harmonious relations in proportion and line in the dress of pupils is now more difficult. But the teacher can at least be an example in this respect, and gradually lead her children to see that anything in a costume which tends to call attention to a defect of person or to exaggerate that defect, anything which tends to center interest where the interest should not be centered, is to be avoided. A good rule is this: Dress so that those who notice your costume will think, "How becoming!" and no one will think, "How expensive!"

VI
SCHOOL WORK A FACTOR

THE teacher who has had but little training in drawing can do much to promote taste and skill through the ordinary work of the schoolroom.

She can lead her pupils to think of appropriate means of expression. A lead pencil and inexpensive, unglazed paper are best for certain exercises; a pen and smooth paper for others; and a brush with ink or water-color for still others. Sometimes a colored crayon will express the truth about some particular object more directly than any other medium. A wise choice of materials with reference to a given end is always a step in the direction of artistic expression.

The teacher can insist on cleanliness and neatness of appearance in all school papers. Children often take an interest in such matters when they see that thumb-marks, dog's-ears, blots, and wrinkles are undesirable simply because they mar the beauty of the sheet. The orderly arrangement of every sheet should be required. Proper margins at left and right, top and bottom, and a balanced page, with the emphasis where it belongs, are of elementary importance, not only in drawing, but in language and number papers, letters, and essays. What is worth doing at all is worth doing well.

This can be enforced by example, through the use of the blackboards by the teacher herself. Blackboards exist for use daily in teaching. They are not supposed to contain elaborate drawings and designs, made more elaborate and hideous by means of colored chalk, preserved from term to term. One small board, or a small portion of a large board, if not needed for other purposes, may contain the school calendar, fresh every month, designed and drawn by one of the children. The honor of placing this calendar on the board should have been secured by winning in a monthly competition. But other designs, such as a portrait surrounded by American flags, and crowned with a spread eagle, a landscape, a bouquet of flowers in color, etc., should not be allowed. The blackboard should not seem to compete with the works of art upon the walls! The blackboard is for rapid illustrative sketches, erased as soon as their immediate usefulness has passed, and for written directions, questions, topics, and problems for the day. These should be well written and well spaced as perpetual reminders of what is expected from pupils. Slovenly boards will be reflected in slovenly papers. By their work the pupils will unconsciously quote Emerson: "What you do" said the seer, " speaks so loudly, I cannot hear what you say."

Several differences between careless and thoughtful written work are shown in Fig. i. The sheet at the top has a margin at one edge for binding, so it is affirmed. The other edge has no margin. The arrangement of matter, not germane to the subject, at the head of the sheet is confusing. The title of the essay is not evident. The whole sheet is unbalanced. In the other sheet balance has been achieved. The title of the essay is isolated, and therefore unmistakable. Name and grade of pupil and date of writing are placed as unobtrusively as possible at the head of the paper. Margins at left and right are equal.To make such a sheet a pupil must think. He cannot begin on the first line and go on heedlessly until the paper is solid full. The making of such a sheet is a problem in design.

If a sheet is not to be bound, extra width of space for binding should not be reserved. The name, grade, and date, if they must come first, would better be smaller or in another color. A better heading would be thus: —

THE STATE OF MAINE
By Harold Green

Longfellow School, Belfast, Gr. VIII Such an arrangement conforms with current practice outside the schoolroom, and is therefore less pedantic.

Figs. 2 and 3 give contrasting pages from school booklets. The first is disorderly. The author's name belongs on the title-page. The initial is out of harmony with the handwriting. The illustration is too large to be used in the text. The arrangement of the text with reference to the picture is puzzling. The margins are absurd. In the second, forethought and good sense, and herefore good taste, are obvious. The illustration is too black, but that is due to the reproduction.

Fig. 4 is from another booklet by a grammar-grade pupil. This booklet was made up almost wholly of quotations from Lincoln and of tributes to him. A more formal hand than the pupil's ordinary writing was therefore appropriate. The arrangement reflects a degree of taste and skill highly creditable to an eighth-grade boy. The verse has the proper form. The title of the picture and the name of the author quoted are in small capitals, hence instantly distinguishable from the text. The picture is rendered so simply that it is in harmony with the writing. It does not appear as a dark, obtrusive spot, like the illustrations upon the pages shown in Fig. 2. The margins are well related to the matter and to the page (whose extent is indicated by the dotted lines). For every kind of paper produced in connection with school topics, there is an appropriate and tasteful form. That form should be the quest of both teacher and pupil. That quest is not promoted by ruled writing-paper, readymade notebooks, and sheets cut 6 by 9. It is promoted by a stock of various kinds of paper, of different colors and textures, in sheets of standard commercial sizes, that children may have the invaluable training afforded by forecasting what they may need, by getting out stock, by working according to plan and specification, and by realizing their own ideals while still in school. Such an experience, oft repeated, is good preparation for life outside the schoolroom.

Tableaux, the folk dance, the drama, and the festival in school life should be welcomed by every lover of beauty, for they offer unprec-edented opportunities for the most intensive training in art and craft in a field which captivates boys and girls and incites them to high endeavor.

VII

SPECIFIC INSTRUCTION A FACTOR UNDER ideal conditions, could they be brought about, specific instruction in visualizing, composing, drawing, coloring, constructing, and perfecting technique, would be given by the teacher in connection with every school topic involving any of these elements. Such a thing as a course of study in art would exist only as a permanent state of mind in the teacher.

It would be like her unwritten course of study in conduct, — a body of habitual practices, based consciously or otherwise on principles of action, to be established in the daily life of her pupils, not so much by precept as by example. But a permanent state of mind of the right sort — combining habitual alertness toward the reports of our senses, with fine reactions upon the data they furnish — is not likely to exist in an uninstructed person. The body of knowledge must be there, however acquired. It may be for the most part subconscious, but there it must be, like the beating heart, influencing every action every day. Moreover, in the teacher the clearer the consciousness of this body of knowledge the better. Her pupils cannot acquire such a body of knowledge all at once. If they acquire it at all it will be by the ancient method. " Precept must be upon precept, precept upon precept; line upon line, line upon line: here a little and there a little" Only the teacher under whose eye the whole realm lies clear will have the wisdom to know which precept to lay to-day upon the precept of yesterday, or which line to add to-day to the line of yesterday, that the paths for thought's hurrying feet may lead to rightness and to peace.

A rough survey of the body of knowledge in art education will be helpful, although that survey be inaccurate and incomplete. The fact is, the realm is not yet fully known. The map reads "Unexplored Region" in several places, and the "Great American Desert" and the "Mountains of the Moon" still exist thereon!

But, laying the figure aside, specific instruction in art education in the elementary schools may be considered, for convenience, under five heads: Color, Plant Drawing (including decorative arrangement), Object Drawing, Design, and Construction (including geometric or working drawings). These divisions of the subject are somewhat arbitrary, but they will serve the present purpose. Under each head seven subdivisions appear. These indicate approximately a developmental order commensurate with a child's growing powers. They may be considered to correspond in a general way with the grades of the elementary school. To be sure, the grades vary in number from seven in some systems to nine in others, the average being eight. The subdivision into seven instead of eight parts is made purposely to suggest the fact that arbitrary grading is undesirable, even were it possible, and that the subject-matter itself should not be too finely sawed and split.

Color Color is one of the three passwords to the world beautiful. The second is Form, and the third Arrangement.

Here the aim of the teacher should be to develop a keenness of the eye for color, a knowledge of pleasing combinations of colors, and skill in producing such combinations.

An orderly procedure, according to present knowledge, seems to be the following: —

(I) *The spectrum* . By means of a glass prism the richest and purest color unit we know is thrown upon a sheet of white paper on the schoolroom wall. It is observed; echoes of it, in the rainbow, dewdrops, fractured ice, glass, flowers, fruits, etc., are recalled; the rainbow stories — "The Flood," "Iris," "Bifrost," "The Pot of Gold," etc., are told. The children begin to search for rainbow colors, collect examples of them, and learn to distinguish five typical colors by name, — red, yellow, green, blue, purple.[6] They discover that these five colors may be arranged in a circuit in the spectrum order, and they learn to think of them in such a relation.

[6] For this advance, the division of the spectrum circuit into five key colors with five intermediate complementary hues, we are indebted to Mr. Albert H. Munsell. See *A Color Notation*, George H. Ellis, Publisher, Boston.

(2) *Typical colors* . By means of natural objects, colored papers, crayons, and water-colors, the five typical colors, their names, and their spectrum order are learned thoroughly as the alphabet of color. By means of experiment with water-colors or crayon the children are led to choose the most pleasing tone of each when used to color a simple design on white paper. They find that the most intense colors are not always the most pleasing and that subdued colors or "middle colors" are found most frequently in nature and in common objects. They discover that usually the brilliant colors are found in small quantities only.

(3) *Values of color* . By experiment with water-colors and by comparison of selected examples the children learn to recognize different values of one color, lighter and darker, and how to pro-duce them by the thinning of the pigment with water, or by adding white for the light values, and by mixing black with the pigment for the dark values. They learn to recognize and to produce the middle red, yellow, green, blue, and purple, and a light and dark value of each. By further experiment they decide the most pleasing combinations of two values of one color in a given design. They are led to see that the two values must not be too near alike, on the one hand, nor, on the other hand, too sharply different. Given a sheet of colored

cover paper, for example, they are required to produce another value of that same color that will look well upon it when used as a booklet cover. Such combinations are called monochromatic harmonies.

(4) *Hues of color* . By observation of natural objects, flowers, leaves, etc., and examples of printed fabrics, and common objects, and by experiment with water-colors, the children are led to see that the typical colors are seldom seen except in school. The greens of grass and of other plants are usually yellower than the typical color green; the reds of autumn leaves are often yellower than the typical red, or sometimes more purple than that red. These varieties of a color are called its hues. Red is now seen to be a family name like Smith or Jones; and Purplish Red, Yellowish Red, etc., thus become names of individual members of the Red family. The children now discover by experiment and observation two hues of color which look well when combined in a given design. They find that the two must not be too much alike, nor very greatly different; that the nearer alike in hue, the more they must differ in value. Given a sheet of colored paper to be used as a booklet cover, they now discover a hue of that color which will look well upon it. Such groups of color are called analogous harmonies.

(5) *Complementary colors* . By experiment the children are led to see that certain colors, — for example a typical color and a hue directly opposite in the pentagonal circuit, — when combined neutralize each other and produce gray. Such colors are said to be complementary. Five typical pairs of such colors are fixed in mind: —

Red	and	the	hue	midway		between G and B called
Blue-Green Yellow	"	"	"	"	"	B " P "
Purple-Blue Green	"	"	"	"	"	P " R "
Red-Purple Blue	"	"	"	"	"	R " Y "
Yellow-Red Purple	"	"	"	"	"	Y " G "

Green-YellowBy experiment with these five pairs of complements children are led to see that pleasing combinations of color may be produced by using complementary colors, provided their relative areas are properly adjusted. One must be dominant, giving its character to the whole design; the two must not vie with each other for first place. Such combinations are called complementary harmonies.

(6) *Chromas or intensities of color* . By observation and experiment the children are now led to see that a color may become grayer without becoming lighter or

darker, and without changing its hue: that is, its chroma may change. They discover and identify colors of weak chroma in the bark of shrubs, in the earth, in polished wood, in textiles, etc., and learn to match these colors and to use them in designs. They discover that colors of weak chroma, when combined with small areas of the same or similar colors of strong chroma, form pleasing groups of harmonious color, either monochromatic, or analogous, or complementary.

(7) *Scales of color* . A scale of colors is any orderly sequence of equal steps. An orderly sequence from white through one color to black constitutes a scale of value, or a monochromatic scale. An orderly sequence from one typical color to another — for example, from red to yellow — constitutes a scale of hues, or an analogous scale. An orderly sequence from one color to its complementary — for example, from blue to yellow-red through gray — constitutes a scale of chromas, or a complementary scale. Such scales (having three or five steps) are made by the children. They learn that the richest color harmonies are often produced by the use of a group of colors from a monochromatic or analogous scale combined with a contrasting color or group of colors from the opposite side of the circuit: for example, tones from a monochromatic scale of purple combined with green-yellow, or a neighboring group of colors or tones from an analogous scale through green combined with red-purple or group of neighboring colors. Such combinations are the so-called "Triads" or complex harmonies. Such harmonies the pupils try to produce in useful objects.

In every use of color from first grade to eighth the aim should be well defined. The pupil should know what he is trying to achieve. In color as in every other phase of art instruction, taste develops gradually through the making of choices with reference to some ideal; and skill through doing things with reference to some standard of excellence. Mere playing with crayons and paints will not insure progress

Plant drawing Because illustrative material in this realm is always available, and because of its rich educational possibilities, plant drawing as the natural accompaniment of nature study should have a large place in the program. Here more easily than elsewhere children can be taught to appreciate Form.

(I) *Growth* . At first, before the color sense is highly developed, and when skill of hand is rudimentary, the children are asked to select the crayon nearest in color to that of the specimen to be drawn — a stalk of grass, let us say. With the green crayon they try to show how the grass grew, — straight or curved; in what direction the leaf grew, whether it is wide or narrow; and what shape the head is. If the specimen is a flower upon its stalk, two colors of crayon are selected, one for the flower and one for the foliage. If characteristic growth and typical color are expressed, the drawing is good.

(2) *Proportions* . The next step is to lead the pupil to observe a little more carefully the relations between the parts. He must now show the relative lengths of stems, leaves, etc., and begin to think of the placing of the drawing upon the sheet so that the whole is pleasing. The size of the drawing must be happily related to the size of the sheet, and the principal part of the drawing so placed that the relative distances from it to the edges of the sheet are agreeable to the eye.

(3) Colors. The aim now is to secure drawings which show, in addition to correct growth, and pleasing proportions, a fidelity in coloring. The hues of color presented in petals, stems, leaves, etc, are now matched as closely as possible. Specific color takes the place of typical color. The children search for variety in color, and express it as faithfully as possible on sheets as well arranged as possible.

(4) *Contours* . Having searched for specific color, the search for specific form is next in order. A good device for isolating the object of quest is a curtain in a sun-lit window, early in the morning. If a spray be placed in a vase or bottle, in direct sunlight, and the window shade be drawn between the observer and the object, the shadow of the object upon the curtain will show in silhouette the exact contours of all the parts, unvexed by detail. Having drawn from the object thus re-duced to two dimensions, the pupil can more easily make such a reduction himself from the object direct. He approaches the object with an informed eye, an eye not so likely to be surprised at the transformations from actual shape to apparent contour brought about by foreshortening. The medium should be the brush, first with ink, and then with any color desired. A low intensity of the typical color of the spray is a good color to use, together with a very delicate tone of the same color used as a background.

(5) *Structure* . Attention is now directed to the anatomy of the plant. Pupils are led to observe closely the details of growth. How stems divide, how leaves are attached to stems, how bud scales and flower petals are arranged, and how leaf blades spring from leaf stalks. Of course such things have not been wholly disregarded in the earlier work; but now they are emphasized. The free rendering of plants for ar-

tistic effect is impossible except on the sound basis of knowledge of the actual facts. Such study yields additional items of interest for use in decorative arrangement, exemplifying harmonies of color.

(6) *Appearance* . The next step leads the pupil to appreciate that growth, proportions, colors, contours, and even the structure itself, when the plant is regarded as a whole, may appear to the eye as something quite different from what they really are. A curved stem may appear straight, a broad leaf may appear narrow, a green leaf catching a reflection may appear blue, an odd contour may resolve itself into leaves and flowers, details of structure may be lost in a glint of light. To represent successfully the appearance of even the simplest spray requires a rather mature power of observation and judgment, and a good deal of skill. The facts discovered through this review of the plant offer hints for new elements and combinations of elements in design.

(6) *Charm* . And lastly pupils are led to see that each kind of plant, even each individual spray, has its own peculiar charm. It may be a grace of gesture (to use Ruskin's phrase), a refinement of line, a harmony of movement through all its parts, a harmony of color, a suggestion of delicacy, strength, wealth of detail, or some unnamable quality of indefinable loveliness. The function of the artist is to discover the particular kind of loveliness the plant displays, and to bring it to the attention of those who love beauty. This calls forth all his resources. He must, with taste and skill, select, compose, ren-der, if he is to make evident to others the beauty he himself sees and enjoys.

In every grade the aim should be sheets which embody the particular aspect of the plant under consideration, with all the taste and skill the pupil possesses at the time. In size and shape, in the position of the drawing within its area, in color, in every detail the sheet should represent the high-water mark of the pupil's power. The revision of the sheet by clipping and mounting is often a profitable exercise when done by the pupil under the direction of a person of, taste. Both arrangement and color effect may sometimes be greatly improved in this way. Such revision affords another opportunity to form a definite judgment with reference to an ideal, and promotes skill.

Object drawing An appreciation of Form, as the second key to the world beautiful, fostered and developed as it may be through the study and representation of plant forms, will not reach maturity without the aid of manufactured objects. Taking hints from nature, man has developed art. The skins of wild beasts may have constituted the first robes, but in process of time they were supplanted by Venetian brocades. Shells and gourds have been displaced by Vaphio cups and Portland vases. Caves have been abandoned for Trianons. Grottoes are forgotten in the dim splendors of Westminster and Notre Dame. The path to the place where one may appreciate these masterpieces of art is called by various names: The first is Scribble and the last is Painting. When children enter the public schools they have, for the most part, left the ill-defined trail through the underbrush, — they have passed the Scribble stage, — and have emerged into the footpath called Imaginative Drawing, which in time becomes the road to Illustration, and the king's highway to Fine Art.

The stages through which one must pass in learning to draw the appearance of common objects seem to be the following: —

(I) *Imaginative drawing* . In this stage, the little artist is hardly more hampered by facts than when in the Scribble stage; and yet there is a difference between the two. In Scribble the few lines which for the child may have had significance at first are confused with other lines without pictorial significance, — just marks, — made, evidently, for the pleasure afforded in seeing them appear as the result of self-will. We never wean ourselves entirely from the pleasure derived from being the cause. From the deepest dungeon of the heart even of a saint where self lies chained, there ascends upon occasion the exultant cry, "I did it with my little hatchet!" But in imaginative drawing, every line and dot is significant; it has a pictorial, or, more strictly, an ideographic value. It represents something, even though it may not to an alien eye look like that thing. Moreover, in this stage solidity is non-existent or conveniently transparent. The child draws the door-knob on the outside of a house, and the hat hanging on a peg inside the house, without the slightest embarrassment. The solid wall between is a baseless fabric in his particular vision. The result is amusing, but the visualizing power it represents is valuable beyond all price. It should be fostered with patient care. Usually it dies, or is allowed to die, or is killed by ridicule. It must be kept alive and brought to maturity, for the possession of it in its fullness means mastership in the realm of the arts.

The aim of the teacher in the lower and primary grades should be to encourage free storytelling by means of drawing of this kind; to insist that every line and dot be significant; and gradually to lead the children to focus their attention more sharply on a few selected subjects, with the determination to represent them more truthfully. Coloring should be realistic.

(2) *Illustrative drawing* . This next stage is characterized by greater thoughtfulness, by more careful selection of subject-matter; in a word, by a larger use of the constructive imagination. Some familiar story is chosen, involving unfamiliar objects. For example, take the story of "Little Red Riding Hood." To tell this story pic-torially, how many scenes must be presented? Certainly two at least, the scene in the wood where the little girl meets the wolf, and the scene in the cottage where she finds the wolf in bed in the place of grandmother. In the earlier stage the child was called upon to reproduce objects with which he had had to do in his own personal experiences. In this stage he is required to image a gloomier forest than he has known, a wolf that in all probability he has never seen alive, a novel headdress for both Red Riding Hood and her grandmother. Moreover, these elements, combined with others of more commonplace character, must be so grouped that the story will be evident, vividly told to every observer.

The aim of the teacher should be to develop clear images and suggestive groupings of the essential objects and their accessories. Nonessentials should be eliminated. The child should realize the picture, get into it, walk about in it, know what is on the other side of things, and have reasons for representing this, and for not representing that. The colors used should be chosen with reference to one another. While the trees of the wood and the blooming plants must have green leaves, and the little girl's hood must be red, a red may be selected that will look well with the green. Emphasis should be placed upon proportions. The story of " Goldilocks and the Three Bears " is an excellent subject for illustration to give practice in judging and recording relative sizes.

(3) *Silhouettes* . This term is used in the largest possible sense, to include not merely the black shadows of objects, but all picturing of objects without special regard to the third dimension. A side view of a toy horse, for example, placed at about the level of the eye, is practically a silhouette, though represented in full color and with considerable fullness of detail. The pupil is encouraged to use his eyes; to see not a horse but this particular horse; to see his true porportions and his

peculiar characteristics. Common objects are observed to discover the position in which they exhibit unmistakably to the eye their true character. A mug turned so that its handle is not seen might be mistaken for a vase of some kind; a front view of a stepladder would not clearly explain itself. Selecting a few common objects likely to be of use in story-telling, the children draw them again and again, using different mediums, crayon, pencil, water-colors, until their correct proportions can be recorded and have been memorized. The children thus begin to collect reliable images of things, the words of the language of graphic expression.

The aim should be the expression of the most important facts concerning the object without wasting time and material. The width and height of a water-pail, for instance, and the number and position of its hoops, are more important than the almost invisible cracks between the staves. The general color of it is more important than the markings of the grain of the wood, or the rivet-heads of the hoops. The medium chosen should be that which, in each particular case, promises to express most directly and adequately the essential character of the object. The easiest and best way for children to represent a tennis racket would be to use a pencil, and to add a wash of color for the wooden frame. To represent a copper kettle, they would better use the brush and water-colors. The character of a Teddybear can be expressed most easily with a crayon.

(4) *The third dimension* . While this has not been wholly ignored in the earlier practice, it now assumes first importance. The children learn the three essentials in a picture: ground, object, and background. They learn to think into the picture with assurance. They discover the various effects of distance: (a) that the farther away, or into the picture, an object is, the smaller it appears; and (b) that the farther away it is, the higher up it must be represented on the paper; and also (c) that the position and size of the drawing, together with the relative areas of ground and background, determine the effect which the picture produces, whether pleasurable or otherwise. Spherical objects are best for first lessons in suggesting this third dimension, for they present the fewest possible difficulties in foreshortening. Hemispherical objects are next in degree of difficulty.

The aim should be the truth of appearance as to size, position, and character of each object, and beauty of space relations upon the sheet.

As in the previous stage, the medium of representation should be thoughtfully selected to express the largest truths in the simplest and most effective way.

(5) *Foreshortening* . The conquest of foreshortened surfaces may well begin with the study of broad leaves seen obliquely. The surprising forms they sometimes assume shock the pupil into seeing. Hemispherical objects may well come next, and then, possibly, rectilinear objects, a book, for example, with its horizontal edges running directly left and right, rather than at an oblique angle with the line of vision. A brush, with two tones of color, one light and one dark, has been proved to be a good medium for the earlier lessons. Cylindrical objects present still further complications, in that the upper face of such an object, being nearer the level of the eye, presents a greater amount of foreshortening than the lower face, a part only of the boundary of which is visible. Rectilinear objects seen at an oblique angle present the most difficulties.

The teacher's aim should be the development of perfectly realized visual images of the objects studied, so that the pupils may be able to draw them at any time from memory. Through constant practice pupils should learn (a) that the more obliquely a face is seen, the more it is foreshortened and the narrower it appears; (b) that this is true whether such faces are below, above, to the left, or to the right of the level and direct line of vision of the eye; and (c) that the long axis of a foreshortened circle, such as the face of a cylinder, is *always* at right angles with the axis of the cylinder. The pencil is the best medium for later studies in foreshortening. When the drawing is correct it may be treated with color, naturalistic or conventional, but always to produce a consistent and pleasing picture.

(6) *Convergence* . In elementary schools mechanical perspective seems to be out of place. Perhaps it is hardly necessary for pupils to know the meaning of horizon line, vanishing point, or any other of the technical terms of the science of perspective. But it is necessary for them to visualize completely rectilinear solids of all sorts, and in various positions, so that all their edges are as well defined to the mind's eye as the visible edges are to the sense of sight. In respect to solidity the accomplished draughtsman has become as the little child. The solid is transparent. Everything is seen with the X-ray. Devices of many kinds have been invented and are advocated to assist pupils in seeing convergence; but in all probability the best device is practice under the guidance of somebody who can draw. Observing, imaging clearly, drawing, and comparing with the object; asking persistently the question," Does the

drawing look like the object? " and answering that question with absolute sincerity; supplementing observation with reasoning and with all the tests of accuracy available, — these are the exercises which lead ultimately to power in delineation.

The aim of teaching and practice should be to secure the conviction, resulting in a sort of automatic reaction through the hand (a) that rectilinear objects present three sets of parallel edges, one set, two sets, or all three sets presenting, whenever they retreat from the eye in any direction, the phenomenon of convergence; (b) that the degree of convergence depends upon the angle at which they retreat; and (c) that retreating horizontal edges always converge toward a point at the level of the eye of the observer.

Undoubtedly the pencil is the best medium in which to make studies in convergence. Color may be added when the drawing is correct.

(7) *Suggestive rendering* . Objects present to the eye other effects than those which may be classified under such headings as Solidity, Foreshortening, and Convergence. A block of wood appears smooth, a hat looks soft, a glass glitters, a stone looks hard and rough. Such qualities cannot be represented by drawing, in the sense that a foreshortened surface can be represented; but they can be suggested by the technique, the manner in which the medium of expression is handled. Suggestive rendering may be achieved in elementary schools by the study of good examples, drawings made by an artist of ability, and especially by watching such a person draw, actually producing before the eyes of the chil-dren the desired object. The power to represent, even to a slight degree, the textures of objects adds greatly to one's delight in drawing, and enhances immeasurably one's capacity for enjoying the works of the masters of pictorial art. The aim in all object-drawing should be to develop the power to visualize, to see clearly with the inner eye the aspect of common objects, and to develop a corresponding power to portray such objects truthfully. At some time almost every adult has been moved to exclaim, "How I wish I could draw!" thus bearing testimony to the value of drawing as a means of expression. Even feeble ability to make use of this graphic language confers a certain distinction and advantage upon him who possesses it, in any trade or profession; and the practice of freehand drawing heightens one's appreciation of pictorial art of every sort.

The sheets produced by pupils in every grade should represent the top-notch of their ability. In emphasis of subject, in thoughtful placing of the object with reference to its frame, and in appropriateness of handling, each drawing should be a work of fine art. Such work will be secured only when children find in the subject something of vital interest, are sure of the steps which lead to successful drawing, are inspired by those who can draw, and are given sufficient time to practice the art until the eye is sure and the hand obedient.

Design

The third key to the world beautiful is Arrangement. A single fish-scale, whatever beauty of color and form it may possess, has little power to awaken an aesthetic emotion; but a large number of scales marshaled in orderly ranks, as they appear upon the body of the fish, does awaken such an emotion. A single crudely drawn black mark has no beauty, but many black marks made by a cunning Greek in orderly sequence in the form of a fret upon the body of his vase may awaken the liveliest aesthetic delight Wild-rose petals fallen in the grass have no less individual beauty than they possessed when growing upon the rose-hip, but the beauty of the flower they constituted is gone, the beauty of arrangement has disappeared. Arrangement in its largest sense is the method of creation and of all the arts. It may be described as an evident order in the parts which constitute the whole. A monotonous order (A) — see Fig. 5 —is the most elementary. A boy running with a stick clattering along a picket fence delights in this elemental repetition. It constitutes the primitive basis of music, and is the order often demanded in the arts, through some sort of necessity; as, for example, in a ladder, a tiled floor, or a chessboard. The accented orders are essentially three: The double movement (B), the basis of "march time"; the triple movement (C), the basis of "waltz time"; and the pentuple movement (D), so frequently met with in nature and in the decorative arts. All other "times" are derived from these or are similar to these in their manifestations. Upon these measures the harmonies of the world arise. To these, the eyes of the children should be opened, that they may see the music of nature and hear the "frozen music" not only of the cathedrals, but of our modern architecture, the shrines of trade. An order of procedure may be somewhat as follows:

(I) *Repetition* . Children already know the meaning of the word. They are first led to see repetition in things about them, — the desks in the schoolroom, the trees along the sidewalk, the petals of a flower. They produce repetition of blocks, lentils, dots, marks. The regular recurrence of the elements may be emphasized by placing to music. With colored crayons the children repeat elements to make borders for their paper napkins, their number papers, nature studies, etc. The aim should be regularity, uni-formity, perfect order, and a result in one color with a neutral.

(2) *Rhythm* . Rhythm is repetition with accent. The simplest form of it is alternation: loud, soft; loud, soft; or long, short; long, short; or bright, dull; bright, dull. The children march to music and without music, to fix the idea. The next rhythm is that of one, two, three; one, two, three; one, two, three. This also is best impressed by means of music and movement. The third rhythmic movement is not often heard in music, but it is often seen in objects. It is best illustrated in the hands. Five elements appear in each, with the accented one, the longest finger, in the center. The children find the same rhythm in the leaf of a wild rose, a woodbine, a maple leaf, etc. They look for all these rhythms elsewhere in nature, and produce them by using lines and other elements drawn with colored pencils. They learn to see that these rhythms occur in one direction, forming borders; in two directions, forming surface patterns; and around a center, forming rosettes. They make use of these kinds of ornament in their school work, particularly their con-structed work.

The aim should be in every case an order that gives pleasure. The coloring should be harmonious. One color and two neutrals, like black and red on a white or manila ground, is safe and effective. All the key colors present great possibilities in such combinations.

(3)*Space division* . The next step is to lead the pupil to see that in an alternation, let us say a flower alternated with a bud in a border, while the alternation itself gives pleasure, the intervals between the units have to be considered. The spaces are elements of beauty as well as the units. One must choose whether the units shall be far apart (E) or near together (F). The same is true, and more evidently true, in a surface pattern, and in a rosette. Moreover, by this time the pupil is old enough to see that the amount of difference between the long and the short in a single "measure" is important. Where ought the cross-line to be placed in an "H"? Where should the title be placed on a book-cover? How much fringe should a rug have, and where should the bands be placed? These, and many other problems in constructive and decorative design, afford opportunity for discrimination, for making those judgments with reference to an ideal which develop taste, and for recording preferences in a way that makes for skill. The aim in every exercise should be space divisions which give pleasure, which seem unimprovable.

(4) *Balance* . Having considered space relations, pupils are ready for that which makes further demands upon the aesthetic judgment, namely, the adjusting of attractions to secure balance. Every line, angle, spot, space, color, in a design constitutes an attraction for the eye; these attractions must be adjusted to give a sense of repose, stability, finality, to the arrangement, whatever it may be. There are two possible adjustments represented by the pan-scale and steelyard, respectively: the bisymmetrical and the free balance. Classic illustrations of these are on a Byzantine panel and a Japanese print. In nature a butterfly and a cockleshell are equally good illustrations. The making of florettes, totems, monograms, and symbolical devices of all sorts appropriate to school or home life, affords ample scope for design at this stage.

The aim should be perfect balance of all attractions so that the eye is satisfied to regard the design as a whole, content with it as it is, assured that each part is of the right shape and color, and in its right place, at peace with all the other elements which constitute its world.

(5) *Adaptation* . Adaptation is the better word for the process known of old as conventionalization. Conventionalization has acquired a restricted and ugly meaning through association with devitalized plant forms. Adaptation is richer in its connotations. It means modifying anything to meet conditions, to fulfill definite requirements. A flower form must be adapted to the cross-stitch, for example, if it is to be used in that kind of embroidery. An animal form — a cat, let us say — must be adapted in shape to fit a circle or a square, and in detail to meet the conditions imposed by the process of printing in one color from a wooden block. Adaptation includes also the fitting of a thing to do its work well, the modification of the parts in view of their function or use. The nose of a pitcher must be adapted to pouring without drooling; a vane must be adapted to the conditions imposed by the wind and those who would know the direction thereof.

The aim is now beauty through perfect adaptation (in addition to all that has gone before). A given result should impress the observer as exhibiting a wise choice of materials, a happy selection of motive, a cleverness in interpreting the natural form into the form appropriate to the materials used, and an appropriate scheme of color.

(6) *Interrelation* . A row of units does not constitute a border; the units must be fused; the individual unit must be subordinate to the group as a whole (compare G and H). In every work of art the same law holds. The whole thing must catch and hold the attention first. If a part — a unit, a space, a color — usurps first place, the harmony is not complete. To secure perfect interrelation of parts is extremely difficult. The interrelation itself may become obtrusive, and thus defeat its purpose. The unity of a white-oak leaf (I) is evident and charming. It is secured through repetition of convex curves, in double measure, on a basis of subtle space division, and a balance that seems bisymmetric, but is really free, and upon a secret but intimate interrelation of all the parts, as indicated by the dotted lines. Some rough approximation to all this must be secured in decorative art that units may become designs. The chief interrelations are: (a) similarity in contours, in the kind of curves bounding the units; (b) similarity in the position of neighboring lines, corresponding with rhyme in poetry; (c) the linking together of certain lines by so adjusting one to another that the eye passes easily, without a jolt, from one element of the design to the next. This corresponds to melody or flow in music and poetry.

"Til the slant yellow beam Down the wood aisle doth seem —"

is poetry. Sidney Lanier's line is in triple time and possesses a melodious flow or succession of syllables, as diagrammed at (J).

"Until the oblique rays of sunlight Down the open spaces in the forest appear —"

is not poetry. It lacks interrelation of parts. Its accented and unaccented syllables succeed one another, as shown at (K), without evident order, and there is no ease of movement for the eye in this, as there is none for the tongue or for the ear in the order of the words.

Pleasing interrelations can be secured only by thoughtful experiment. They are so important that they should be considered at the very outset in planning the design and the units adapted to them. One advantage of "free design," with "abstract spots" as units, is, that beginning with a group of meaningless spots, by means of experiments with tracing-paper, these interrelations may be discovered. The design may be built upon them without any consideration of such limitations as a definite area to be filled, a given size and shape of repeat to be used, a particular flower shape to be kept, of recognizable form and yet adapted to the conditions imposed by a certain material and technique. But alas, these are the perpetual problems of the practical designer. They cannot be ignored in effective school work.

The aim in designing should be consistency of pattern, the holding together of all the elements, a vital whole in which each part takes its own proper place in relation to all the other parts.

(7) *Style* Style means congruity or consistency in the quality of the elements employed, in all their relations to one another, in their adaptation to the material, in their appropriateness to the occasion, and in their reflection of the personality of the designer. For pupils in elementary schools style means consistency in treatment of handling. A design may be stiff and mechanical like an Egyptian fret, or sinuous and freehand like a flamboyant Gothic capital, or strong and temperate like a Greek palmette, or vigorous and luxuriant like a Roman frieze of acanthus scrolls; but in any case it must appear such throughout. One part must not be elephantine and another serpentine, or one part a meaningless empty desert while another is a wilderness of confused detail. Style is promoted by the use of a single material, tool, or medium, or as near an approach to that as may be. A border of cut paper is better than a border partly cut and partly drawn. A bit of embroidery all textile in quality is better than a stenciled pattern where threads and paint vie with each other for first place. A design drawn with a pencil throughout is likely to be better in effect than a design in which various qualities of line appear. If two mediums are employed, one must be given such prominence that it dominates the other and plays chief part in the effect. The aim should be harmony, a condition where nothing can be added and nothing removed to improve the effect; a condition where all the elements conspire to produce in a person of taste a sense of satisfaction with the whole.

In every grade the practice of designing should be preceded and supplemented by practice in observing applied design. The children should be led to acquire the habit of coming to a decision as to the excellence of every bit of decoration they see. That their decision be right or wrong is not so important as that it be made. In the presence of decorated things of any kind, — handkerchiefs with ornamented borders, figured dress goods, rugs, wall-papers, embroidered curtains, scarfs, collars, decorated china, inlaid floors, carved wood or stone, — they should habitually decide whether the ornament seems to them to be appropriate and excellent, or otherwise, and why. By such decisions, supplemented by actual practice of decoration in the simple things they make, they will come to finer taste and greater skill in design.

Construction

Construction means the production of things in tangible form. In school work such activities as drawing by means of ruler and compass, working to scale, directly involved in the process of producing things, are classed under this head. Construction is the logical conclusion of design. Construction tests the adequacy of drawing. Con-struction reveals the limitations and possibilities of materials as to both form and color. Without construction art is likely to become fantastic, insincere, and impractical.

A separate course in construction is quite as undesirable as a separate course in drawing or in design unrelated to school and home activities. Moreover, such a course would tend to become quickly a mechanical and formal course, without life or beauty of result. From the very first, therefore, drawing, designing, and coloring should eventuate in construction. The supposition that in any given grade but one kind of constructive material ought to be allowed, or that there should be a "course" in the use of any particular material like paper, raffia, or wood, seems to be a mistake. The "course" should consist of projects vital to the daily life of the children. If in the working-out of these projects paper or cloth or leather or metal is required it should be used forthwith, and manipulated as well as the skill of the pupil will allow. And yet experience has taught that it is possible and advisable to make use in school of such vital projects, in each grade, as lay emphasis upon the materials and processes generally amenable to the powers of the children of that grade. For example, projects involving the use of woodworking tools would better not be attempted with primary children; metalwork is of doubtful expediency below the high school; modeling, while advantageous to pupils of every grade, seems to hold especially rich educational possibilities for first-grade children.

Experience has taught still further that in the constructive process certain elements are always present guiding or at least influencing the activities of the craftsman. An idea is to be embodied; the object must be of definite width and height, of pleasing proportions; the nature of the material employed must be reflected, and the technique obviously appropriate to the character of that material; the make of the object throughout, its plan, structure, and workmanship, must be adequate and skillful, if the object is to give satisfaction to all concerned. These four elements should influence all school work in construction, each in turn receiving special emphasis as the developing powers of the children make such emphasis intelligible and fruitful.

In the light of the foregoing considerations the seven headings which follow, indicating in a general way the dominant points for emphasis in successive grades, and appropriate materials, tools, and processes, may not be misinterpreted.

(I) *Embodying* the idea. In construction as in object drawing, free expression must precede trained expression. During the first weeks in school the spontaneous constructive activities of the home life, such as building with blocks, playing with sand, making boxhouses for dolls, mud pies for the fun of it, begin to take on greater significance through the use of building-blocks, the sand-table, the kindergarten "gifts," and plastic material for modeling. At first the teacher will be satisfied if the building be purposeful, if a definite plan be worked out in whatever is attempted, if the idea be evidently embodied in the result of modeling and making. Of course the work will be exceedingly crude so far as technical qualities are concerned; but such qualities are of slight importance compared with the quality of life. The questions are, Does the thing seem vital? Is it charged with purpose? Does it manifest the thing it was intended to manifest? Has the little worker caught the idea and expressed it in his work? If so, the result is to be commended no matter how crude it may be.

(2) *Determining proportions* . That dolls are as tall as forest trees, that doors are coextensive with whole front walls of play-houses, that a toy chair is wider than it is high, is not at first of the slightest consequence to children. As the mind develops, such incongruities become evident and undesirable. Things begin to be seen in other than mere narrative relation. The mind demands measure and proportion. The children now begin to cut paper and cardboard to definite size and shape; the ruler is introduced to determine lengths and widths. Things are made of predetermined proportions. Results begin to be judged upon the basis of excellence in form. Common flat objects, like sheets of notepaper and envelopes to correspond, tags, signal flags, and such things as toy sleds, chairs, and utensils of various sorts, which

may be cut flat and folded into shape, are examples of projects appropriate to this stage of development.

(3) *Relating to material* . Presently the children discover that paper sleds are not as praiseworthy as wooden sleds; that while a paper may-basket will do for temporary use, a school bag is better when made of cloth. In other words, they arrive at the place where relations between use and material are perceived. As soon as they attempt to make a thing in wood or cloth that they made previously in paper, they discover that certain modifications are necessary. The material helps to determine the make. Perhaps the conditions imposed by material and process are no better exemplified than in weaving. Certainly weaving is a form of constructive art which appeals to children in the middle grades of the elementary school. The planning of something to be woven, a little rug, a school bag, or a basket, the laying-out of the pattern on squared paper to discover the number of threads or weavers and how they must be related to make the stripe or figure, the weaving, strand by strand, are all educative processes of the highest value, fruitful in taste and skill.

(4) *Building* But things in the flat soon fail to satisfy the growing powers. The weaving of a basket whets the appetite for making other things in the round, such as boxes, toys, and useful objects of various kinds, requiring but few tools. The demand for related views of the object to be constructed now becomes evident. Children learn to use the compasses, to draw to scale, to make working drawings involving plan and elevation, to get out parts and to assemble them to build a whole. The embodiment of the idea, in a form of pleasing proportions in which appropriate material is wisely handled with a fair degree of skill, is a possible achievement on the part of well-instructed children from ten to thirteen years of age.

(5) *Making in cloth and leather* . As appreciation of the æsthetic element in common things increases, projects should be chosen which admit of richer decoration, and which require, in the making, greater skill of hand. Objects involving nee dlework for the girls, and the use of the leather-tooling kit for the boys, have proved valuable at this stage. The boys need not be denied the use of the scissors and needle, nor the girls the use of the knife and burnisher; but sometimes a general division in constructive work seems now desirable. Good designs for needlework or tool-work cannot be made without experience in actual working-out in the material. Here theory and practice react on each other to the advantage of the craftsman

and his product Projects of immediate interest to children, useful things to be worn or put to daily use, such as collars, cuffs, ornamental bands, belts, fobs, cardcases, pocket-books, and the like, offer alluring possibilities, not only for expressing one's best thought as to appropriate form, but one's best feeling for harmonious color.

6) *Dressmaking and woodworking* . The projects now become more complicated, requiring a sustained interest and persistence in working for more remote ends. The girls make doll's clothing, and then some garment for themselves. The boys make mechanical toys, and then some simple piece of furniture for the home. Working with patterns, and from drawings or blueprints, basting, stitching, embroidering, handling successfully the common tools of the carpenter at the bench, — these are some of the activities peculiarly appropriate to the upper grammar grades. One or two projects should be carried through to completion in the pupil's best manner. His work should represent the high-water mark of his intelligence and skill. The danger here is in attempting too much. An attainable goal is more stimulating to boys and girls than an unattainable vision in the clouds.

(7) *Printing and bookbinding* . The type-case and the printing-press are be-coming more widely recognized every day as efficient instruments in manual arts education. Through printing, a large number of common school topics — spelling, language work, English composition, mathematics, drawing, design, color, etc.— are vitalized and interrelated to a useful end, immediately rec-ognizable as such by young and old alike. Bookbinding is the logical conclusion. Its requirements are exacting; its field unlimited in the direction of fine craftsmanship. The equipment for such crafts is somewhat expensive at first, but the running expense is not great; and the results amply justify the cost. In schools where proper equipment is not available, good training in many of the essential elements of these crafts may be secured through the practice of pen-lettering, and the making of objects involving the use of the simpler bookbinding tools. Motto-cards, menus, place-cards, telephone rosters, desk pads, portfolios, booklets, and other useful objects capable of giving pleasure through excellence of design and workmanship, offer unlimited scope to the powers of pupils of the upper grammar grades.

The teacher should keep constantly in mind that to make a thing is not so important as to make a desired thing; and that to make a desired thing is not so important educationally as to make it rightly. Constructive activities should be so directed that the children acquire the habit of approaching problems auspiciously, that is, in a way that gives promise of success. The pupil's first question in the presence of any constructive problem should be, What is required? Having determined that fully, the next question is, How can the conditions be met adequately, in a pleasing manner? And the third is, To what extent can I reveal my own taste and skill, my own love of beauty, through the work of my own hands?

VIII
THE TEACHER THE CHIEF FACTOR

BUT after any analysis of the educational problem, no matter how fruitful the result may be, or may promise to be, the broad-minded and candid observer must admit that ultimately the sine qua rum is always found to be the teacher. A seed may appear perfect under the microscope, contain every material element in due proportion, and yet be dead, incapable of sprouting. The essential thing in the seed that is to produce a harvest is life. A live teacher will always produce living fruit, whatever the material elements may be with which he must work.

In the realm of art education the teacher and his personal equipment seem to be of transcendent importance. Dr. Emerson E. White was fond of saying, "An art is caught, not taught." Here is a bit of first-hand testimony on this point from one who is now a successful supervisor of drawing:—

As a boy at school, I had one teacher who drew. He drew incessantly and drew well. Thinking back to it now, I realize that he drew practically everything known to our little world. He illustrated his arithmetic and physiology, drew continually in his geography classes, and made history a downright delight by depicting not only the positions of the infantry, cavalry, etc., but also the various kinds of uniforms, accouterments, and ordnance; and I well remember how we cheered when the splendid galleons of the Armada went to pieces on our blackboard just as they did in 1588 off the English coast.

But our greatest interest centered in his hobby — Natural History. Here he seemed preeminent; and we observed the remarkable structure of the woodpecker's tongue, or noted the points of difference between the wildcat and the lynx, from the lucid and accurate drawings which appeared before us.

We did not know that we were learning to draw. We would not have called it drawing anyway. It was simply that we gradually came to express ourselves as he did.

Masters of pedagogy may say whatsoever they will; I, for one, believe there is no better theory of teaching art than the homely old one of imitation. Teachers who draw put sand on the tracks, so to speak, the wheels grip the rails afresh, and their pupils swiftly enter new and hitherto unsuspected realms of power[6].

The teacher who can draw possesses undoubtedly an enviable advantage in teaching. But art education means far more than teaching children to draw. The teacher who possesses a fair degree of taste; who exemplifies in himself the art of applying a knowledge of form and color harmonies in dress and personal adornment; who is not content until every feature of his schoolroom is of such a character that it may contribute its share in the educational process; who insists that his pupils, in all they do, live up to all the light they have, and work at their highest possible level of efficiency, as he himself does; and above all a teacher Who in addition has a brooding love for the boys and girls under his charge, and a perpetual enthusiasm for fine things, will be sure to achieve success in giving to his pupils an appreciation for the beautiful and a power to produce beautiful things.

EMERSON.

---

6   From an article by Paul £. Beck, in the School *Arts Magazine*, May, 1913.

" Day by day for her darlings To her much she added more; In her hundred-gated Thebes Every chamber was a door, A door to something grander, — Loftier walls and vaster floor."

The Codes Of Hammurabi And Moses
W. W. Davies

QTY

The discovery of the Hammurabi Code is one of the greatest achievements of archaeology, and is of paramount interest, not only to the student of the Bible, but also to all those interested in ancient history...

Religion   **ISBN:** *1-59462-338-4*   **Pages:132**
MSRP $12.95

The Theory of Moral Sentiments
Adam Smith

QTY

This work from 1749. contains original theories of conscience amd moral judgment and it is the foundation for systemof morals.

Philosophy   ISBN: *1-59462-777-0*   **Pages:536**
MSRP $19.95

Jessica's First Prayer
Hesba Stretton

QTY

In a screened and secluded corner of one of the many railway-bridges which span the streets of London there could be seen a few years ago, from five o'clock every morning until half past eight, a tidily set-out coffee-stall, consisting of a trestle and board, upon which stood two large tin cans, with a small fire of charcoal burning under each so as to keep the coffee boiling during the early hours of the morning when the work-people were thronging into the city on their way to their daily toil...

Pages:84

Childrens   ISBN: *1-59462-373-2*   *MSRP $9.95*

My Life and Work
Henry Ford

QTY

Henry Ford revolutionized the world with his implementation of mass production for the Model T automobile. Gain valuable business insight into his life and work with his own auto-biography... "We have only started on our development of our country we have not as yet, with all our talk of wonderful progress, done more than scratch the surface. The progress has been wonderful enough but..."

Pages:300

Biographies/   ISBN: *1-59462-198-5*   *MSRP $21.95*

FRANCIS WELLMAN

The Art of Cross-Examination
Francis Wellman

QTY

I presume it is the experience of every author, after his first book is published upon an important subject, to be almost overwhelmed with a wealth of ideas and illustrations which could readily have been included in his book, and which to his own mind, at least, seem to make a second edition inevitable. Such certainly was the case with me; and when the first edition had reached its sixth impression in five months, I rejoiced to learn that it seemed to my publishers that the book had met with a sufficiently favorable reception to justify a second and considerably enlarged edition. ..

Pages:412

Reference   ISBN: *1-59462-647-2*   *MSRP $19.95*

On the Duty of Civil Disobedience
Henry David Thoreau

QTY

Thoreau wrote his famous essay, On the Duty of Civil Disobedience, as a protest against an unjust but popular war and the immoral but popular institution of slave-owning. He did more than write—he declined to pay his taxes, and was hauled off to gaol in consequence. Who can say how much this refusal of his hastened the end of the war and of slavery ?

Law   ISBN: *1-59462-747-9*   **Pages:48**

MSRP $7.45

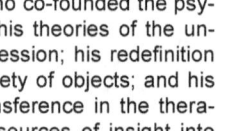

Dream Psychology
Psychoanalysis for Beginners

Sigmund Freud

Dream Psychology Psychoanalysis for Beginners
Sigmund Freud

QTY

Sigmund Freud, born Sigismund Schlomo Freud (May 6, 1856 - September 23, 1939), was a Jewish-Austrian neurologist and psychiatrist who co-founded the psychoanalytic school of psychology. Freud is best known for his theories of the unconscious mind, especially involving the mechanism of repression; his redefinition of sexual desire as mobile and directed towards a wide variety of objects; and his therapeutic techniques, especially his understanding of transference in the therapeutic relationship and the presumed value of dreams as sources of insight into unconscious desires.

Pages:196

Psychology   ISBN: *1-59462-905-6*   *MSRP $15.45*

The Miracle of Right Thought
Orison Swett Marden

QTY

Believe with all of your heart that you will do what you were made to do. When the mind has once formed the habit of holding cheerful, happy, prosperous pictures, it will not be easy to form the opposite habit. It does not matter how improbable or how far away this realization may see, or how dark the prospects may be, if we visualize them as best we can, as vividly as possible, hold tenaciously to them and vigorously struggle to attain them, they will gradually become actualized, realized in the life. But a desire, a longing without endeavor, a yearning abandoned or held indifferently will vanish without realization.

Pages:360

Self Help   ISBN: *1-59462-644-8*   *MSRP $25.45*

The Rosicrucian Cosmo-Conception Mystic Christianity *by Max Heindel* ISBN: *1-59462-188-8* **$38.95**
The Rosicrucian Cosmo-conception is not dogmatic, neither does it appeal to any other authority than the reason of the student. It is: not controversial, but is: sent forth in the, hope that it may help to clear... New Age/Religion Pages 646

Abandonment To Divine Providence *by Jean-Pierre de Caussade* ISBN: *1-59462-228-0* **$25.95**
"The Rev. Jean Pierre de Caussade was one of the most remarkable spiritual writers of the Society of Jesus in France in the 18th Century. His death took place at Toulouse in 1751. His works have gone through many editions and have been republished... Inspirational/Religion Pages 400

Mental Chemistry *by Charles Haanel* ISBN: *1-59462-192-6* **$23.95**
Mental Chemistry allows the change of material conditions by combining and appropriately utilizing the power of the mind. Much like applied chemistry creates something new and unique out of careful combinations of chemicals the mastery of mental chemistry... New Age Pages 354

The Letters of Robert Browning and Elizabeth Barret Barrett 1845-1846 vol II ISBN: *1-59462-193-4* **$35.95**
by Robert Browning and Elizabeth Barrett Biographies Pages 596

Gleanings In Genesis (volume I) *by Arthur W. Pink* ISBN: *1-59462-130-6* **$27.45**
Appropriately has Genesis been termed "the seed plot of the Bible" for in it we have, in germ form, almost all of the great doctrines which are afterwards fully developed in the books of Scripture which follow... Religion/Inspirational Pages 420

The Master Key *by L. W. de Laurence* ISBN: *1-59462-001-6* **$30.95**
In no branch of human knowledge has there been a more lively increase of the spirit of research during the past few years than in the study of Psychology, Concentration and Mental Discipline. The requests for authentic lessons in Thought Control, Mental Discipline and... New Age/Business Pages 422

The Lesser Key Of Solomon Goetia *by L. W. de Laurence* ISBN: *1-59462-092-X* **$9.95**
This translation of the first book of the "Lernegton" which is now for the first time made accessible to students of Talismanic Magic was done, after careful collation and edition, from numerous Ancient Manuscripts in Hebrew, Latin, and French... New Age/Occult Pages 92

Rubaiyat Of Omar Khayyam *by Edward Fitzgerald* ISBN:*1-59462-332-5* **$13.95**
Edward Fitzgerald, whom the world has already learned, in spite of his own efforts to remain within the shadow of anonymity, to look upon as one of the rarest poets of the century, was born at Bredfield, in Suffolk, on the 31st of March, 1809. He was the third son of John Purcell... Music Pages 172

Ancient Law *by Henry Maine* ISBN: *1-59462-128-4* **$29.95**
The chief object of the following pages is to indicate some of the earliest ideas of mankind, as they are reflected in Ancient Law, and to point out the relation of those ideas to modern thought. Religiom/History Pages 452

Far-Away Stories *by William J. Locke* ISBN: *1-59462-129-2* **$19.45**
"Good wine needs no bush, but a collection of mixed vintages does. And this book is just such a collection. Some of the stories I do not want to remain buried for ever in the museum files of dead magazine-numbers an author's not unpardonable vanity..." Fiction Pages 272

Life of David Crockett *by David Crockett* ISBN: *1-59462-250-7* **$27.45**
"Colonel David Crockett was one of the most remarkable men of the times in which he lived. Born in humble life, but gifted with a strong will, an indomitable courage, and unremitting perseverance... Biographies/New Age Pages 424

Lip-Reading *by Edward Nitchie* ISBN: *1-59462-206-X* **$25.95**
Edward B. Nitchie, founder of the New York School for the Hard of Hearing, now the Nitchie School of Lip-Reading, Inc, wrote "LIP-READING Principles and Practice". The development and perfecting of this meritorious work on lip-reading was an undertaking... How-to Pages 400

A Handbook of Suggestive Therapeutics, Applied Hypnotism, Psychic Science ISBN: *1-59462-214-0* **$24.95**
by Henry Munro Health/New Age/Health/Self-help Pages 376

A Doll's House: and Two Other Plays *by Henrik Ibsen* ISBN: *1-59462-112-8* **$19.95**
Henrik Ibsen created this classic when in revolutionary 1848 Rome. Introducing some striking concepts in playwriting for the realist genre, this play has been studied the world over. Fiction/Classics/Plays 308

The Light of Asia *by sir Edwin Arnold* ISBN: *1-59462-204-3* **$13.95**
In this poetic masterpiece, Edwin Arnold describes the life and teachings of Buddha. The man who was to become known as Buddha to the world was born as Prince Gautama of India but he rejected the worldly riches and abandoned the reigns of power when... Religion/History/Biographies Pages 170

The Complete Works of Guy de Maupassant *by Guy de Maupassant* ISBN: *1-59462-157-8* **$16.95**
"For days and days, nights and nights, I had dreamed of that first kiss which was to consecrate our engagement, and I knew not on what spot I should put my lips..." Fiction/Classics Pages 240

The Art of Cross-Examination *by Francis L. Wellman* ISBN: *1-59462-309-0* **$26.95**
Written by a renowned trial lawyer, Wellman imparts his experience and uses case studies to explain how to use psychology to extract desired information through questioning. How-to/Science/Reference Pages 408

Answered or Unanswered? *by Louisa Vaughan* ISBN: *1-59462-248-5* **$10.95**
Miracles of Faith in China Religion Pages 112

The Edinburgh Lectures on Mental Science (1909) *by Thomas* ISBN: *1-59462-008-3* **$11.95**
This book contains the substance of a course of lectures recently given by the writer in the Queen Street Hall, Edinburgh. Its purpose is to indicate the Natural Principles governing the relation between Mental Action and Material Conditions... New Age/Psychology Pages 148

Ayesha *by H. Rider Haggard* ISBN: *1-59462-301-5* **$24.95**
Verily and indeed it is the unexpected that happens! Probably if there was one person upon the earth from whom the Editor of this, and of a certain previous history, did not expect to hear again... Classics Pages 380

Ayala's Angel *by Anthony Trollope* ISBN: *1-59462-352-X* **$29.95**
The two girls were both pretty, but Lucy who was twenty-one who supposed to be simple and comparatively unattractive, whereas Ayala was credited, as her Bombwhat romantic name might show, with poetic charm and a taste for romance. Ayala when her father died was nineteen... Fiction Pages 484

The American Commonwealth *by James Bryce* ISBN: *1-59462-286-8* **$34.45**
An interpretation of American democratic political theory. It examines political mechanics and society from the perspective of Scotsman James Bryce Politics Pages 572

Stories of the Pilgrims *by Margaret P. Pumphrey* ISBN: *1-59462-116-0* **$17.95**
This book explores pilgrims religious oppression in England as well as their escape to Holland and eventual crossing to America on the Mayflower, and their early days in New England... History Pages 268

QTY

The Fasting Cure *by Sinclair Upton*   ISBN: *1-59462-222-1* **$13.95**

In the Cosmopolitan Magazine for May, 1910, and in the Contemporary Review (London) for April, 1910, I published an article dealing with my experiences in fasting. I have written a great many magazine articles, but never one which attracted so much attention... New Age/Self Help/Health Pages 164

Hebrew Astrology *by Sepharial*   ISBN: *1-59462-308-2* **$13.45**

In these days of advanced thinking it is a matter of common observation that we have left many of the old landmarks behind and that we are now pressing forward to greater heights and to a wider horizon than that which represented the mind-content of our progenitors... Astrology Pages 144

Thought Vibration or The Law of Attraction in the Thought World   ISBN: *1-59462-127-6* **$12.95**

by William Walker Atkinson   *Psychology/Religion Pages 144*

Optimism *by Helen Keller*   ISBN: *1-59462-108-X* **$15.95**

Helen Keller was blind, deaf, and mute since 19 months old, yet famously learned how to overcome these handicaps, communicate with the world, and spread her lectures promoting optimism. An inspiring read for everyone... Biographies/Inspirational Pages 84

Sara Crewe *by Frances Burnett*   ISBN: *1-59462-360-0* **$9.45**

In the first place, Miss Minchin lived in London. Her home was a large, dull, tall one, in a large, dull square, where all the houses were alike, and all the sparrows were alike, and where all the door-knockers made the same heavy sound... Childrens/Classic Pages 88

The Autobiography of Benjamin Franklin *by Benjamin Franklin*   ISBN: *1-59462-135-7* **$24.95**

The Autobiography of Benjamin Franklin has probably been more extensively read than any other American historical work, and no other book of its kind has had such ups and downs of fortune. Franklin lived for many years in England, where he was agent... Biographies/History Pages 332

Name	
Email	
Telephone	
Address	
City, State ZIP	

☐ **Credit Card**   ☐ **Check / Money Order**

Credit Card Number	
Expiration Date	
Signature	

Please Mail to: Book Jungle
PO Box 2226
Champaign, IL 61825
or Fax to: 630-214-0564